Dear Parents,

Welcome to the Scholastic Reader series. We have taken over 80 years of experience with teachers, parents, and children and put it into a program that is designed to match your child's interests and skills.

Level 1—Short sentences and stories made up of words kids can sound out using their phonics skills and words that are important to remember.

Level 2—Longer sentences and stories with words kids need to know and new "big" words that they will want to know.

Level 3—From sentences to paragraphs to longer stories, these books have large "chunks" of texts and are made up of a rich vocabulary.

Level 4—First chapter books with more words and fewer pictures.

It is important that children learn to read well enough to succeed in school and beyond. Here are ideas for reading this book with your child:

- Look at the book together. Encourage your child to read the title and make a prediction about the story.
- Read the book together. Encourage your child to sound out words when appropriate. When your child struggles, you can help by providing the word.
- Encourage your child to retell the story. This is a great way to check for comprehension.
- Have your child take the fluency test on the last page to check progress.

Scholastic Readers are designed to support your child's efforts to learn how to read at every age and every stage. Enjoy helping your child learn to read and love to read.

— **Francie Alexander**
  Chief Education Officer
  Scholastic Education

For Luke and Lila, Justin and Ian
—A.S.

To my dear friends... Bud and Evelyne Johnson
—L.D.

Copyright © 1995 by Scholastic Inc.
The activities on pages 27-32 copyright © 1995 by Marilyn Burns.
Fluency activities copyright © 2004 Scholastic Inc.
All rights reserved. Published by Scholastic Inc.
SCHOLASTIC, CARTWHEEL BOOKS, and associated logos
are trademarks and/or registered trademarks of Scholastic Inc.

Library of Congress Cataloging-in-Publication Data is available.

ISBN: 0-590-18074-6

10 9 8 7 6 5   07 08
Printed in the U.S.A. 23 • First printing, October 1995

SLOWER THAN A SNAIL

by **Anne Schreiber**

Illustrated by **Larry Daste**

Math Activities by **Marilyn Burns**

Scholastic Reader — Level 2

SCHOLASTIC INC.

New York   Toronto   London   Auckland   Sydney
Mexico City   New Delhi   Hong Kong   Buenos Aires

"Hurry up! You're slower than a snail!"

"Slower than a snail? No way!" I wailed.

"I'm smaller than an elephant.
I'm bigger than a poodle.

I'm shorter than a rocket ship.
I'm longer than a noodle.

I'm wider than a string bean.
I'm narrower than a truck.

I'm lighter than a ton of bricks.

I'm heavier than a duck.

Skyscrapers rise above me.
Tunnels are below.
It's easy to size things up.
I just use what I know!

I'm longer than a shoelace.
I'm shorter than this guy.

I'm smaller than an airplane.
I'm bigger than a fly.

I'm taller than a monkey.
I'm shorter than a tree.

I'm smaller than a rainbow.
I'm bigger than a flea.

I'm larger than some things.
I'm smaller than others.
But there is one thing
I am not, my big brother ...

and that's slower
than a snail."

• ABOUT THE ACTIVITIES •

Sorting, comparing, and classifying objects in different ways is valuable preparation for children learning about number, measurement, and shape. Children are interested in investigating objects and naturally compare them. For example, they may classify things by whether they are big or little. "That glass is little." "My doll is big." "The package is too big for me to carry."

Later, children become aware of different physical properties of objects. Their observations and comparisons become more precise as they look for relationships between objects. "Your glass holds more than mine." "My doll is taller than yours." "The package is too heavy for me."

The activities and games in this section build on the comparisons made in the story. Some use pictures; some use common objects you might have on hand. The directions are written for you to read along with your child.

Children may enjoy doing their favorite activities again and again. Encourage them to do so. Or try a different activity at each reading. Be open to your child's interests, and have fun with math!

— Marilyn Burns

You'll find tips and suggestions
for guiding the activities whenever
you see a box like this!

Retelling the Story

The little girl said she was smaller than an elephant. You are, too. What other animals are you smaller than?

The girl also said she was bigger than a poodle. Are you? What else are you bigger than?

Reread the story. Think of other things that could be in it.

As you reread the story, stop so you and your child can think of substitutions for the comparisons. Listen to your child's ideas and offer some of your own. Be playful!

A Sorting Box

Collect objects and put them in a box.

> Try to collect about 20 objects. They can all be the same, such as buttons or keys. Or you can combine objects — buttons, keys, nails, jar lids, nuts, bolts, coins, pebbles, etc. Let your child examine the objects and play with them. Then introduce the sorting activities.

Pick out one object from the box. Tell just one thing about it. You might say that it is round or white or bumpy or something else. But tell just one thing.

Take out all the other objects in the box that are round or white or bumpy or whatever. Put them in a pile.

Then put everything back in the box and play again with another object.

Point to something near the girl.

Point to something far from the girl.

Point to something on top of the girl.

Point to something underneath the girl.

Point to something smaller than the girl.

Point to something larger than the girl.

Point to something taller than the girl.

Point to something shorter than the girl.

What Do I See?

Find picture pairs to solve the riddles.

I see something long, something short.
I see something round, something square.
I see something that is big, something little.
I see something that is tall, something short.
I see something that is wide, something thin.

Can you make up other picture-pair riddles?